Angel Dust

POEMS & SHORT STORIES

Tatterdemalion Blue

First published by **Tatterdemalion** Blue in 2015

Words © Cristina Mureşan 2015
Illustrations © Gisele Moura 2015

Illustrations by Kind Permission - Gisele Moura

A CIP catalogue record for this book is available from the British Library

Cover design and layout by **Tatterdemalion** Blue

ISBN 978-0-9933114-2-0

Tatterdemalion Blue
8 Upper Bridge Street
Stirling
FK8 1ER

www.tatterdemalionblue.com

Angel Dust

POEMS & SHORT STORIES

Cristina Mureşan

Cristina Mureşan, Ph.D., wrote her first poem when she was six years old. Actually, she couldn't write yet, so she dictated it to her father. It was a two-page poem about the four seasons. In the years that followed she started a career in public relations, completed a doctorate in international relations and traveled the world. Through 'Angel Dust', her first book, she hopes to share some of the magic she encountered along the way. The poems and short stories are inspired by her travels, her rich inner world and spirituality.

for my mother
who always encouraged me to write
for my father
who always supported me

CONTENTS

POEMS

SHORT STORIES

Angel Dust

POEMS

SEARCH FOR BEAUTY

Oh, traveler of endless roads
Searching for beauty in love and truth
Beauty of kindness and inspiration
Beauty of shapes and beauty of colors
Get drenched in the loveliness of a smile
Let the splendor of a flower enchant you
Allow the magic of a loving gaze run through you
And through your trials and your revelations
Remember it is not beauty that lives in you
It is you who lives in beauty.

INSPIRATION

I listen closely
And the words come to me
Already spoken by a different mouth
Already written by a different hand
Like a sculpture hidden in the stone
Or the music behind the silence
The words travel to find me
Through space and time
And where we meet is inspiration.

WORDS

There is an ocean of words in me
Words released from the trap
Of my doubts and fears
Words that want to fly like birds
Around the earth
To tell the story of my heart
My journey in this world
A moment in time, a feeling I felt
And the beauty I have seen
They are all in me, like birds
Waiting to fly.

THE POET

The master of all poets
Is sitting on his ancient stone
Having mastery over words
He is always silent
Knowing the essence of all things
He sees no difference
Between a grain of sand
And the whole universe
If he were to tell his story
He wouldn't know where to start
For his story has no beginning or end
If he were to speak
He would speak in riddles
For more than a poet
He is the lord of love
And more than a master
He is a father.

THE ARTIST

Let your colors be painted
Let your melody be sung
Let your words give new meanings
Let the wings of your inspiration grow
And above all, let your light shine
You only have yourself to give.

MAGIC

I weave a carpet
With strings of my soul
Sometimes, I take strings
From the soul of the world
To make a flying carpet
The magic carpet
That takes us
To an enchanted land.

RIVER OF LIFE

In this flow of people and places
I stand still, while carried away
In the endless movement of life
Do I give a gift to the world?
Or is the world a gift to me?

THE INNER MOUNTAIN

Climbing that inner mountain
My soul is one with
As the ego twists and turns
I am finally free.

HONEY DUST

See the sky, starry and fair
Feel the nectar fill the air
Golden light will never fade
Heaven is always, honey made.

MUSE CAFÉ

Pearls of wisdom, words of pain,
Drops of silence, sounds of rain,
Playful musings, tears in vain,
Joyful verses, let love reign.

WEB OF LIFE

Golden river through a deep canyon
Holy water rushing to its source
I am merely a stop in your journey
I hope my boat will catch your tide
Run through my veins
Connect me to the whole
Written it is in the great book of life
We are all one.

(IM)MORTALITY

I would be in this moment forever
And always speak as if
These were my last words
I would look at the world
As if it was for the last time
I would keep my promises
I would fulfill my prophecies
As if I were never to die
As if I were never to live.

QUEEN OF HEARTS

There will be a time
When all people will think of their hearts
And the heart of their hearts
Then everyone will think of all the others
Until they will know of only one
A huge beautiful heart
The queen of all hearts
And people will never have to say
They are looking for a heart of gold
For gold will pale in comparison
People will never have to say
Let our hearts beat as one
As there will be only one heart
Beating.

SPIRIT

Stardust blown through my being
Boundless awareness through space and time
A cosmic dance only inner eyes can see
A truth only the magic mirror can reflect
Eternal stillness
Ultimate freedom
I am.

ETERNITY

I sit at your doorstep
Gazing into the unknown
Yet so familiar
You watch me closely
Not a single breath you miss
Not a single movement escapes you
Tides of love flowing
Space and time colliding
This is eternity.

PILGRIMAGE

I wanted to pay you a visit
And then I realized
That you visit me
Every second of every day
When you continuously walk
Through the doors of my being
Where am I to look for you?
On the top of the mountain
Or down in the valley?
In the forest or by the sea?
You visit me eternally
For I belong to you.

THE MASTER

Teach me, love me, guide me
When I am ready come and meet me
Patience, gravity and truth
Master, help me find my roots
Be with me, don't let me fall
In the end I will find my home
I am you and you are me
A most ancient mystery.

TREASURE

You may be a king or a queen
Adorned with gold and pearls
Wear shiny clothes and diamonds
But when you knock at the doors
Of your inner kingdom
When you walk on the path
Of your soul-searching
When your eyes marvel
At the joy of self-discovery
Wear your jewelry inside
Shine your gold in your heart
Sparkle your soul like a diamond
Adorn yourself with the beauty of love
Seek the treasure behind the treasure.

INTEGRATION

Up and down, black and white,
Yin and Yang, left and right,
Make them one, make them you,
Turn to unity, be true,
Wrong or right, darkness and light,
Be a master, win the fight,
Hell and heaven, war and peace,
Keep the balance, stay in bliss.

AWAKENED SPIRIT

Oh, dormant god
For ages lost in your majestic sleep
Adorned with golden dreams
So close in distant stillness
As your enemies are conquered
Open your eyes.

WORSHIP

Let me turn my breath into the breath of life
My glance into the light of love
Let me turn my silence into the sound of joy
My stillness into a cosmic swirl
My every breath into a prayer.

THE GIFT OF LOVE

I come empty handed
I don't carry any gifts
What could I ever give you
When you already have all of me?
I come empty handed
For I know you will give me
The greatest gift of all
And if my hand is empty
It is only because my heart is free.

OPEN HEART

What would you do
If your heart outgrew you?
What if it was so big
That it was no longer in you
Instead, you are in it
As a small piece of a puzzle
Only beginning to unravel?
People say only the reckless
Carry their heart in their hand
But what if your heart carried you?
What if it were to float around you
A gentle, yet powerful presence
Slowly encompassing the whole world?

GRACE

You fill my cup
You make me dance
You walk through me
Amazing grace.

MAGICAL RAIN

Your love will melt me
I will turn into a drop of water
Then I will turn into a cloud
Then I will rain on you.

THE FLUTE

If I were to have something
It would be the kind of love
That moves mountains
If I were to receive a gift
I would want it to be
The gift of sweetness
Yet nothing I have
I came into this world
Empty as a flute
But I hope when I leave
The flute will be playing
A beautiful melody.

SAMSARA

Mighty wheel ever turning
Endless cycles of life and death
The eyes of your soul
See it all in slow motion
The smile in your heart
Proves it is all a dream
If you want to rewrite the story
You must know thyself.

GOLDEN ARMOUR

Covered from head to toe
With my golden armour of bliss
I don't feel invincible
I feel at home.

SNOWFLAKE

Do not be afraid, little snowflake
If you melt, you will be a drop of water
If you evaporate, you will be a cloud
You will be transformed, yet unchanged
You will be what you were born to be
A drop in the ocean of life.

HOPE

Sweet child of my sweet mother,
When you stray, or when you wander,
When you fail, when you lose,
If you're lost, if you're confused,
Remember it can be better.

Sweet sister, sweet brother,
See yourself, there is no other,
If you're strong, or if you're weak,
When all is night, when all is bleak,
Remember it can be better.

Sweet guardian angel, sweet lover,
Send me hope, help me discover,
All the wonders that I seek,
Let winds blow, caress my cheek,
You know it can be better.

SILENCE

When words fail to express
The intensity of feelings
When thoughts are poor vehicles
To communicate the depth of vision
Return to the vibrant silence in your heart
Find the sacred space between sounds
And from that magical place
Look back at the indescribable
Contemplate the inexpressible
Merge with the silence
Beyond the silence.

DEVOTION

With every step engraved in stone,
I love you every day much more,
I love you deep, I love you wide,
I love you to the moon and sky,
From the soft wind and mighty ocean,
I take the strength of my devotion.

FAITH

You came to me in the midst of turmoil
From the jungle of my sorrows
I could barely see your light
You slayed the demons of my ignorance
On the darkest paths of my soul
You brought the fire of love
So I could see my true self
And let go of my pain
With a voice softer than a breeze
Yet more powerful than thunder
You said you came for me
And I believed.

TREASURE HUNT

Would you search for diamonds
If you were to shine even brighter?
Would you dig for gold
With golden tools?
My fellow traveler, my friend
I will not stop you from your quest
I will merely point you to a mirror
Whose reflection will show you
The treasure you've been searching for.

IMPRINTED

Imprinted in eternity
I watch the silence
I move along with
The ever changing winds
Blowing over ancient peaks.

GRATITUDE

If the perfume of a thousand roses
Turned into liquid
And ran through my veins
It would be nothing compared to
The fragrance of a blissful heart
Pumping gratitude with every beat.

THE WANDERING TRAVELER

You say you have been walking forever
The dusty roads of your soul searching
Where would you long to go
If you knew you had the world inside?
When your restlessness turns into peace
And magic comes to your door
Your wanderings will become epic tales
And you will no longer be a traveler
But a gardener, with the world as a backyard.

FLEETING GRACE

The loveliness of a flower lasts for a season
The magic of a butterfly enchants for one day
The wonder of a shooting star vanishes in a blink
Fleeting moments of grace become gentle reminders
Of a place where flowers' blooming is everlasting
And where butterflies turn into shooting stars
Once their day has come to an end
Some might call it heaven.

GOLDEN AGE

Great warriors under the guise of gentle poets
Lion-hearts in peaceful eyes of householders
Kings and queens of humble working hands
Powerful masters behind sweet children's smiles
In the radiance of a new irrepressible dawn
They point their shiny arrows towards the darkness
They write the long forgotten songs of freedom
They rise in much awaited love supreme.

TRANSFORMATION

If your soul feels like an old house
Covered with the spider webs
Of your own dark thoughts
If your heart is like
A once beautiful garden
Now invaded by thorns
Sometimes all it takes
Is a soft ray of sunshine
Through your dusty window
Or the song of a nightingale
Above your tired trees
For the breath of life
To change thorns into roses
And make old things new.

HOME

People say a house
Can only become a home
With the love that fills it
Some say home is a bond
That can never be broken
Or the food that never goes cold
They say if you carry your home with you
You will be as slow as the snail
But I have learned
That he who finds home in his heart
Will offer shelter to the whole world.

CONNECTION

There is no distance
Between you and me
The flesh and the skin
The spaces among us
Are not really there
We are all connected
By invisible strings
We make a huge body
Who is aware
We are all a part of it
It is us who forget.

MOTHER EARTH

Learn from the trees
Bending just enough
To endure strong winds
Learn from the roots
Going around the stone
To reach the source of water
Learn from the birds
Who find their way
Across long distances
Be soft, yet solid
Like the earth.

ODE TO WATER

I am made of water
It permeates the whole of me
My body and my soul
I am made of water
The mildest thing
The strongest thing
A great master once said
Water is the carrier of divine love
And like the soul of water
I carry life, I carry love
Holy water, hallowed be thy name
For I am made of you.

TREACHEROUS SEA

On an island
Surrounded by
A treacherous sea
Navigate your boat
Carefully, knowing
It is now or never
The time of greatest
Blessings, as well as
The time of greatest
Struggles, the time for
Giving the best of you.

THE LOTUS

Born of mud but standing high
Growing up towards the sky
Graceful, colorful and fragrant
Flawless beauty sent from heaven
Like the spirit deep within
Spreading fragrance through our being.

SPRING

The air was filled with blissful scents
I walked in awe, a smile on my face
I felt so very lucky to have seen
The loveliest spring that had ever been.

Could have walked forever that night
With all around, alive and bright
The trees in bloom, with open arms
Gave all they had, gave all their charm.

My soul unfolded in waves and flowers
My eyes were filled with mystic waters
A symphony of joy, life did bring
The night I fell in love, with Lady Spring.

CHANGE

Unstoppable, change
Never comes without
A ruthless struggle
Between old and new
How could an ancient wall
Hold a powerful torrent
For longer than a blink?
The endless blink of a tired
Yet unforgiving eye
Of soon forgotten eras.

REVOLUTION

When having is more important than becoming
When words no longer enlighten but enslave
When the old smothers the new
It is time to start a revolution from within
The dissolution of all doubts and fears
Allowing the winds of change to blow freely
Through sleeping minds and sleeping streets
Making all things new.

THE LOST UNICORN

Shooting stars and angels
Unicorns and rainbows
Fairies, mighty wizards
Gods and daunting demons
Long forgotten worlds
Splendor beyond words
Come in dreams at night
Make the darkness bright.

ANGEL'S DREAM

I once saw the world
Through the eyes of an angel
It was as beautiful
As the first fall of snow
For a moment I thought
I was an angel too
And then joy burst
Through my every pore
And I remembered.

HEART AND SOUL

The Soul said to the Heart,
"You always lead me into trouble."
The Heart smiled and said,
"Sometimes I trouble your waters
To bring up what lies underneath."
"Heart of mine, you make me work so hard,
Climbing the highest mountains,
Crossing the deepest seas."
"I want you to see the world,
So you have a story to tell," said the Heart.
"People say I should listen to you,
But sometimes I can't hear you," uttered the soul.
"If you dance, my music will begin to play,"
Said the Heart.

DREAMS

A wise man once said to me
Stay far from daydreaming
Or you might dream your life away
Another wise man said
Never trust a petty mind's dreams
Or you might lose your soul for ever
The wisest of them all said to me
Believe in dreams born of a pure heart
And they might dream you back into life.

WILD CHILD

Wild child, wild flower,
Hidden beauty, hidden power,
Dream and play like there is no other,
Bring infinity into your every hour.

TWIST OF FATE

Try it once, think twice,
Peaceful mind, cool as ice,
Reckless heart, play nice,
If you run, you will pay the price,
Cats will always chase the mice,
Faith, as small as grain of rice,
Fills with love your own device.

SEEKER OF TRUTH

I am an echo of my true self
A reflection of the essence
A glimpse of an ancient memory
A haunting, ever-growing longing
For a hidden, mysterious smile
A deep, primordial seeking
For the lost, golden flame.

WARRIOR OF PURE HEART

Blazing spear in your hand
Shining armor, foe or friend?
Deadly strength lies in your arm
Blade as cold as the heart is warm
Rivals and enemies alike
You could break with just one strike
If you slay them, though in glory
They will never know your story.

SEA OF LOVE

Sailing on the seas of the heart
Steering through storms and calm waters
Finding safety in hidden harbors
Will not bring your boat back home.

AS IF

Walk as if you are already
Where you want to be
Let your destination
Be one with your journey.

ROMEOS AND JULIETS

When there is no fear and there is no doubt
When anger is missing and hate is thrown out
Head over heels, to the other devout
Their love to the world, with one voice, they shout.

When there is no death and their love not outdone
When pain is a myth and eternity could be won
Their love will unite all hearts under the sun
Their sacrifice will remind us, that we are all one.

THE SWORD

I feel you resting in my hand
I know you are both foe and friend
You have always been a part of me
I never thought without you, I could be.

If I dissolve my anger and my fear
Then I no longer need that spear
Loving the enemy is not easy
By loving him, you know him deeply.

I am becoming sweet and mild
My sword will now become my child
Though born in darkness and confusion
We are turning into light now, no illusion.

The foe united with the friend
The sword no longer in my hand
Forever it will be a part of me
My foe and friend, my child it will be.

TWO FATHERS

Two fathers, two kings
One grounds you, one gives you wings
United in their love for a child
Born of one, raised by the other
They are different, yet the same
Two sides of a coin, rulers of the game
One is the source, the other the path
Behold their smile, beware their wrath
Always far, yet always near
Realising your dreams, dissolving your fears.

LOST AND FOUND

Sometimes I get lost in the world
Until I find the world in me
Sometimes I lose all freedom
Until I become truly liberated
Sometimes I have to lose it all
To reinvent my secret garden.

CITY OF LIFE

In a city where roads are rivers
People carry their hearts in their hands
They float as if they were one
With the rivers that are never dry
They have the kind of love
Coming from a heart always open
A heart as gentle as the waters.

In a city where roads are veins
Linked to the heart of the universe
People are never tired, nor old
The sun would always shine
Taking its light from the people's eyes
The music would always play
Taking its melody from life itself.

In a city where bridges are rainbows
People are at home everywhere they go
Rivers are kind and hearts are warm
The rain would make people dance
The wind would be the breath of life
The clouds would be storytellers
The skies would be life's open gates.

COLORS OF LIFE

Smile with the sun, cry into the rain,
Walk over the rainbow, dance away the pain,
Fire up the heart, cleanse the soul in snow,
Dream along the stars, let the magic flow.

CHILD OF THE FIRE

Give your soul to the fire
Let it burn and pass the test
Consumed by the flames
The gold is renewed.

ANGEL CHILD

Splendid creature, made of light
Shining more than stars shine bright
I am not yours, you are not mine
Love me until the end of time
Where you came from, I wish I knew
Angel's steps are my heart's dew
I am not scared, fly with me
Let it be what is meant to be.

FREEDOM

When you're so far away
From your comfort zone
That it looks like a dot
You can be sure that
Magic is about to begin
When you think so much
Outside of your box
That it's as big as the sky
Your mind is finally free.

WAVES OF CHANGE

Surfing the waves of change
Mastering the powerful currents
Yet letting your self be surprised
Stand up on that surfboard and smile
There is only your self to account to.

THE PATH

Go where you have to go
Do what you have to do
And fear will take care of itself
Find your voice in silence.

PEARLS

Some people are like seashells
Hard outside, soft inside
The tiniest drop of sand may disturb them
Yet sometimes they are able
To turn it into a pearl.

THE MAGICIAN

Dusty roads and heavy feet
Until his heart and mind will meet
Endless search for love and glory
Magic will rewrite his story.

DEEP WATERS

If your soul were an ocean
Would you let me swim in it?
I would dive with mermaids
I would surf your waves
I would be stranded on an island
Caressed by your sun.

THE WOMAN

The beauty of her face
Is only matched
By the beauty of her heart
She can be as fierce
As she can be gentle
She embodies both
The mother of all the mothers
And the daughter of all daughters
While she is alive
The world would be afraid
That it might be outdone
When she dies
The world itself will feel like dying
For a piece of the soul of the world
Would have gone with her.

WINTER DREAM

One night I had the fairest dream
While angels were all sleeping still
Three wise men marching in the cold
To bring frankincense, myrrh and gold
I see them carrying precious gifts
Their gold shines bright and darkness lifts
Their peace and joy makes me feel whole
Their myrrh somehow comforts my soul
They said
"Behold, beware and believe
It all comes true on Christmas Eve."

EASTER DAY

We break the eggs to break into a new life
We unlock our narrow minds to be free
We let go of our old selves to get new meaning
We pray for the grace to pervade our being
We eat the bread of knowledge
We drink the wine of love
We light the candles of joy
We bow before the Saviour
Whose love knows no boundaries
Whose radiance removes the darkness
Whose grace consumes our sins
We kneel in prayer
We gather in joy
We unite in freedom.

POWER OF ELEMENTS

Will the fire burn you
Or will it make you radiant?
Will the earth swallow you
Or will it ground you?
Will the water dissolve you
Or will it make you penetrating?
Will the wind blow you away
Or will it expand you?

UNIVERSALITY

I am alone, yet I have
The universe inside
If I breathe, my breath
Is one with the wind?

HEART CONNECTION

Coated in my own soul
I am connected to
The soul of the world
Wrapped in my heart
I feel the heart of the universe.

SWEET POISON

Drinking my tears, drinking my pain
Sometimes the world turns without me
Sometimes giving brings no gain
I wish I could rewind the sands of time
So what I lost, could for a moment be mine.

But then I sit still and look deep within me
I open my heart, I let the world turn
And remember what life could and should be
I may drink poison, yet in the end I will be free
All melts away, inside I am made of eternity.

TIMELESS ECHO

Your love will move my mountains
My love will part your sea
My water will flow in your fountains
Your light will shine in me
And if all else fails
And if all else falls
I will still love you forever
Wherever our fate calls.

THE POTTER

His strong hands master the secret
Of the empty vessels filled with love
His eyes endlessly seek for ways
To contain emptiness in a cup
His cups are made ready to collect
What they were always meant to.

TIME

Time is precious, how time flies
Life is crazy, love is blind
Joy and pain, in words that rhyme
Grateful is this heart of mine
While empires rise and fall
Big today, tomorrow small
Present, future or the past
Love is first, love is last.

SHORT STORIES

SOMEWHERE UNDER THE RAINBOW

Nina was a journalist who had always been fond of traveling. She must have been in hundreds of planes, trains, buses or cars. She deeply believed in the saying, "Those who don't believe in magic will never find it," therefore she tried to keep her mind and heart open to whatever magic was out there waiting for her in the world. That day she was on a plane, traveling to attend a friend's wedding. Nina was seated by the window, eager to see the world from above. She always loved being above the clouds; they reminded her of fresh snow, but a bit closer to the heavens. Seated next to her was a little girl, about the age of 6 or 7, traveling with her mom. Soon after the plane took off, the little girl's mother fell asleep, leaving her busy with a coloring book. Nina was lost in her thoughts, so she didn't pay much attention to her little neighbor.

At a certain moment during the flight, the captain announced a storm, all passengers were advised to stay in their seats. The rain soon cleared and the plane was above the clouds again, under a bright sun.

Suddenly, Nina saw one of the most amazing things she ever witnessed. A huge rainbow appeared very close to the plane, she felt as if she could reach out and touch it. She loved rainbows, and felt they were part of the magic she was so fascinated with. Nina must have seen hundreds of them all around the world, but this one had something special: it was really close, closer than any other rainbow ever was. This time, not only could she witness the magic, it was almost as if she could be part of it. "If there was ever a movie called 'Magical world', this could be the making of it," she thought to herself smiling.

"It's made of angel dust, you know," a little voice spoke.

"I'm sorry, what did you say?"

"Angel dust ... it's what rainbows are made of," Nina's little neighbor said.

"Oh, I see. And what is that?"

"It's like fairy dust, but for angels. There's a special angel that picks it from the angels' wings. It's a mixture of fairy dust and stardust, but much more powerful. That's why it's called angel dust."

Nina's eyes were sparkling with excitement. She felt like a little girl again, playing in a secret garden with her best friend.

"I wish we had some angel dust too," Nina said. "So we can make our own rainbows whenever we want."

"We will, when our wings are fully grown," the little girl said, in a very serious tone.

"What's your name, darling?"

"Sara."

"I'm Nina. So, Sara, what did you mean about those wings? I thought only birds or ... angels have them."

"We all have them, but we forgot. Until they are fully grown again, we are angels with growing wings. Only when they are fully grown, we can fly. Until we can fly, no dust can come on our wings. We have to wait until then to make our own angel dust."

"And who told you all these things, Sara?"

"No one. I just figured it out on my own."

"Ahem. So how is angel dust different than fairy dust?"

"It's different because it has magic, like fairy dust, but it also has some more angels' stuff in it ... like love and hope ... Santa Claus's sleigh is also made of angel dust ... and maybe dolphins too, but I'm not sure ..."

"Sara, are you bothering people again with your stories?" the little girl's mother said covering her yawn.

"Oh, it's okay," Nina said, "I really enjoyed her company. Your daughter has a wonderful imagination."

"You're so kind, she probably read too many fairytales if you ask me," the lady said. "Oh, look at the time, I must have slept for quite a while ... we're landing soon."

"You missed an amazing rainbow before," Nina continued.

"Oh, there will be other rainbows."

"I guess ... this one was very special though ... we passed right under it. Never saw one so close before," Nina said, more to herself.

"That's nice," the lady said. "Sara, put down

your coloring book, we're preparing for landing soon."

And soon enough, the plane landed, and everyone rushed out to find their luggage. Just before losing sight of her, Nina waved and smiled to Sara.

"Don't forget to grow your wings," Sara said, with the same serious tone she had carried the whole conversation with.

Nina was left with a smile on her face, a light in her eyes and a silent joy in her heart. Out of all the rainbows, and all the plane rides, this was definitely the most unforgettable. It was as if she had passed under a rainbow, on a magic carpet ... made of angel dust.

A DAY WITH THE GANGES

Once upon a time, a saint, now in Heaven, wanted to return to earth just for one day, to enjoy the company of the River Ganges. First, he decided to take the form of a river stone. He was sitting motionless on the bottom of the Ganges, while the sparkling waters were gently flowing all around him. The Ganges was telling him many interesting things. She was speaking of the people who bathed in her waters, of their stories and prayers. She was whispering about the ashes of those who wanted to join the holy river after they had departed from earth, about their lives and their destinies.

The saint was listening and enjoying the fascinating tales of the people who had touched the Ganges, and who were now imprinted in the memory of her waters. The river was flowing around the saint and through his being while he was silently observing the animals and people bathing close by.

After a while, the saint, feeling he was one with the Ganges, took the form of a small leaf floating along wherever the river was taking him. The saint was joyous, as he was caressed by the sun and carried along beautiful landscapes. He saw deep jungles, ancient cities and colorful villages. The Ganges was glad to have such an honored guest and wanted to show him everything.

Suddenly, a fish rushed and quickly swallowed the small floating leaf. Soon after, a fisherman caught the fish and took it home on the riverbanks of the Ganges. The fisherman's wife gutted and scaled the fish her husband brought home that day, and threw the scraps back into the river, together with the small leaf.

What a journey!

The saint was pleased to have seen a picture of himself inside the fisherman's modest hut. Their family had been worshippers of the saint for generations. Unknown to them, the saint had visited their home, rejoiced in their love for him and blessed the family again and again.

The small leaf was now floating on the Ganges, contemplating the beauty all around. The sun was about to set, and a lovely pink light was enveloping the entire landscape. It was the perfect ending to a great day as the guest of the River Ganges.

Just before sunset, the leaf was drawn into a waterfall, and fell again into eternity.

TWO SOULS

Two souls were sitting on the shores of Life.

"... we'll soon descend on earth and begin our journey. You'll have to be patient with me, you know how I am, I may be delayed ... " the First Soul said.

In response, the Second Soul smiled silently.

"... and when I finally arrive, it will be as if I've just reached home, but I can't find my key to open the door ..." the First Soul continued.

"... so you might try to break the door ..." the Second Soul added.

"... only to find the door will reject me, to teach me to accept myself ..."

"... you may even try and go through the back door ..." the Second Soul continued.

"... but that might deprive me of the warm welcome ..." the First Soul said.

"... I bet you'll start crying in front of the door like a lost child ..." the Second Soul said gently, "... but eventually you'll remember you actually have the key and you'll just have to work to open the door ..."

"... so the keyword would be 'work', a labor of love ..." the First Soul said and smiled with a twinkle in her eyes.

"... yes, but in that process, you might discover the door was open all along ..." the Second Soul uttered.

"... or that the door is actually a mirror ..." the First Soul continued.

"... and? ..." the Second Soul asked.

"... and I may need to look at myself in this mirror before going inside ..." the First Soul replied.

"... or maybe it's like a treasure hunt ..." the Second Soul declared.

"... a treasure hunt for the treasure that I already have but forgot I did? ..." the First Soul said.

"... well, yes, and you'll look for it everywhere ..."

"... everywhere but inside myself, where it would have been all along ..." the First Soul concluded delicately.

A peaceful silence emerged between the two souls. They were smiling in anticipation. It would be a long journey, but it would be unforgettable.

"... and then? ..." the First Soul asked.

"... let ourselves be surprised, we'll write the story as it goes ..." the Second Soul said.

"... so we'll be the writers, the directors and the actors too? ..." the First Soul asked in amused disbelief.

"... we'll do it as Shakespeare taught us ..."

"... who's Shakespeare? ..."

"... remember that bright soul that we met yesterday? He was saying he had become quite good at doing this down there. He used to be called Shakespeare, and he was trying to give clues to people for their own treasure hunts ..."

"... oh, yes! I remember! His class was pretty good. We promised to pay him a visit when we're back, and tell him how we used his lessons ..." the First Soul said laughing.

"... we'll probably be in time for tea tomorrow, but with all your detours we may end up going to dinner after all, you know how time flies down there ..." the Second Soul laughed back.

"... he's busy with all the other souls he's

coaching. He won't even notice we're late ..."

"... just remember, I may not always hold your hand, but I'll always be holding your heart ..." the Second Soul said after a moment of thoughtful silence.

"... I'll try to remember ..." the First Soul replied, a smile on her face.

"... in joy we start, but there might be a few tears along the way ..." warned the Second Soul.

"... you know laughter and tears will be part of the deal, but sometimes you have to endure the rain to see a rainbow afterwards ..."

"... so are you ready? ..."

"... you go first. I still have time for a deep breath ..." the First Soul spoke sweetly.

"... farewell! ..." the Second Soul said and disappeared with a smile on his face.

"... so let the play begin ..." the First Soul said to herself. "... for, as Shakespeare told us: "All the world's a stage, and all the men and women merely players. They have their exits and their entrances" ..."

The First Soul contemplated the Sea of Life for a second, with the clarity of distance and a concern about the final outcome.

"... it's time ..." she thought to herself, before vanishing into the great waterfall of joys, sorrows, love, laughter and tears, called Life.

It was indeed time for a new adventure and this one would definitely be out of the ordinary.

THE GARDENER

A rose tree was blooming its heart out in a beautiful garden. A traveler passing by on the road stopped near the rose tree, amazed at its beauty. Enchanted by the scent of the roses, the traveler reached to pick a flower.

"Mind your hand, traveler! My flowers have thorns," warned the rose tree. "Only the gardener may pick my flowers. He spends his days attending to me and he has the tools to cut my flowers so that my thorns won't prick him."

"Forgive me, I didn't know," answered the traveler. "But aren't you afraid your flowers will die when the gardener cuts them?"

"I can always grow more flowers," said the rose tree, "but I want to adorn my gardener's house. I'm here to bring him joy."

"You are very generous with him," said the traveler.

"I wouldn't exist without him. He knows my rhythms. In winter when I have neither leaves nor flowers, we both wait patiently for the spring to come again. Every year my flowers are more beautiful and my fragrance is stronger because of his care."

"Your gardener must be very proud," continued the traveler.

"All I see is his smile while he quenches my thirst. All I hear is the song he sings while he picks the weed around me. While others love me for themselves, he loves me for myself."

"Would you mind if I smell your flowers?" inquired the traveler.

"That I won't mind. And know that while you travel your endless roads, you will marvel at the beauty of many gardens and you will be charmed by the perfume of their flowers. And one day you will grow your own garden."

"Not everyone is a gardener," replied the traveler.

"Everyone is a gardener ... they just don't know it yet," whispered the rose tree while a gush of wind blew its scent all across the road, leaving the traveler on its path, a smile on his face and a song in his heart.

THE DRAGONFLY

Based on a true story

One warm, sunny summer day, Anna was taking a bath in the river. She had been in a mountain camp during the school holiday for over a week. The surroundings were beautiful and Anna was feeling peaceful and connected to everything around her. The river was quite cold, but she didn't mind. It was refreshing. She was alone, sitting on a river stone, her feet in the water and her face caressed by the sun. She loved the nature sounds all around her and the smell of the forest nearby. Everything seemed so alive and magical.

Suddenly, something blue and bright caught Anna's eye. A pair of big blue dragonflies were flying around her, as if dancing in the air. Their wings were shining under the sun and their intense blue was fascinating. Anna couldn't take her eyes off of them. For a brief moment, without even realizing it, she thought to herself: "I wish I had wings like that." Her impossible desire made her smile, but she was so relaxed that her reasoning wasn't able to censor her thought. Soon enough, the dragonflies disappeared and Anna continued her daydreaming. Later on, when she was ready to leave, she stood up and turned around. She almost cried with amazement when she saw a pair of blue dragonfly wings on a nearby stone. Anna couldn't believe her own eyes. It felt like a dream. She looked around to see a trace of the dragonflies, dead or alive, but there was none. She took the wings in her hand and looked at them closely. They looked as if they were made of the most delicate lace in the world. "Lace made by fairies," Anna thought. Almost unable to believe her luck, yet grateful for this gift, she took the wings with her and kept them safe until she finally returned home a few days later.

She decided to keep the wings in a small wooden box. She enjoyed looking at them once in a while. It made her smile and reminded her that magic existed. She also remembered some of the fairytales her grandmother used to tell her when she was little. Stories from the Eastern European mythology, about the Queen of Bees or the Queen of Ants who were saved from danger by the hero of the story. In return, the hero was granted one of the Queen's wings, with a promise that whenever in danger, if they burned the wing, she would come to their rescue.

Years passed and Anna kept the wings hoping that one day, if ever she needed it, she would get help from the Queen of Dragonflies. And even if that was just a story, it was too beautiful not to keep it in a corner of her heart. Anna had always been a dreamer and a believer. She wasn't naive, but she made a conscious choice to see true magic where others saw only superstition. She thought true magic was much like true love, the more you believe in it, the more it manifests.

More than ten years later, Anna had grown to be a writer and was now living in London. She was struggling to get her first book published. After many rejections from many publishers, she was feeling almost ready to give it all up. She had forgotten about the dragonfly wings and magic. And yet throughout the years, she had always carried them with her, in their wooden box, wherever she went.

One day she was cleaning some drawers and she stumbled upon the small wooden box that had the dragonfly wings inside. She was upset and disappointed by all the rejections from the publishers. Seeing the wings again made her smile and even if a part of her was skeptical, she felt now was the time to call upon help from the Queen of Dragonflies. "It can't hurt," Anna thought to herself, "I've tried everything. Even if magic and myths won't help me, at least it might be fun to try and it will keep my mind off my problems for a while."

So the next day she took the wings with her and she went for a walk in the beautiful area of Hampstead, where she lived. It was a space inhabited by many artists and she loved walking around, whenever she was in search of inspiration. She decided to let her creative spirit guide her and let things flow.

She was looking for a place where she could burn one of the dragonfly wings, walking around like a child in a treasure hunt. Her mind slowly became peaceful and once again, as she did when she was a child, she immersed herself in the present moment.

Her heart opened and she felt in tune with everything around her. Her mind became more receptive and her senses became sharper. She remembered an old church she used to love as it was very quiet. When she got there, she went behind the church, next to a small side entrance on top of a few stairs. She sat down on the stairs and took a deep breath. Then she took one of the wings out of the box and lit it up. She was very excited, yet very peaceful.

She closed her eyes for a few seconds praying for guidance. When she opened them, something bright caught her eye. A woman was passing by and her hair ornament was shining under the sun. The woman appeared to walk as if in slow motion and Anna saw, to her amazement, that her hair ornament was in fact a big silver dragonfly. She only saw it for a second but without any hesitation, she stood up and followed the woman through the narrow streets of Hampstead. At one point, at a crossroads, she almost lost sight of her and Anna's heart started pounding. She started running and barely saw the woman as she entered into a shop.

It was a vintage shop Anna had seen before. She rushed in but there was no trace of the woman anywhere. "Maybe she went through another door," Anna thought, "and as I was quite far away I thought it was this shop."

While she was struggling with her own mind, blaming herself for not being more alert, a man approached her and asked:

"Do you want to buy that shawl?"

"Pardon?" said Anna.

"The shawl you are looking at … do you want to buy it? Because if you don't, I'm interested."

Without realizing it, Anna had picked up a shawl in her hand, but she had been so lost in her thoughts that she hadn't been aware she was still holding on to it.

"No, sorry, I was just looking. It's all yours," she mumbled.

"Oh, your accent is very interesting. Are you Spanish?" asked the man.

"No, I come from Romania, Transylvania," Anna said. "But somehow everyone in London thinks

I'm Italian."

"Interesting," said the man, laughing. "I've been to Transylvania. Beautiful place. And what do you do in London?"

"I'm a writer. I'm trying to publish my first book."

"Any luck so far?"

"Not really, it's been quite a nightmare," Anna said in low voice.

"I'm a writer too," said the man. "I have published a few books and then I decided to start my own publishing company."

"Oh really?" Anna said, cautiously excited.

"Yes, I'm always looking for young talents. Maybe I can help."

Anna examined the man for a second, trying to see if he was serious. He seemed a very respectable gentleman, well dressed, with a kind smile on his face.

"Maybe we should have coffee one day. I'll give you my card," said the man. "I would invite you right now, but I'm waiting for my wife who went to have a word with the shop owner. Oh, there she is!"

"Hello," a woman's voice said.

"Hello," said Anna and turned around to see, much to her amazement, that the man's wife was in fact the woman she had been chasing around Hampstead, wearing a dragonfly ornament in her hair.

The woman and Anna smiled at each other. And even if the woman wasn't the Queen of Dragonflies, in that moment, Anna knew that magic was always alive.

Sure enough, the kind gentleman would later help her to publish her book, and Anna became good friends with his wife. Who was very fond of dragonflies and was always delighted to hear a story about a little girl who sat at the river daydreaming and was given two dragonfly wings as a gift. But more than just the help from the Queen of Dragonflies, the wings would be a reminder that she could fly herself, as far as her spirit would take her.

CAST AWAY

A Postmodern Fairytale

In a kingdom far away, there lived a princess called Hope. She was beautiful and charming and everyone loved her: her family, her friends and her subjects. She had everything and she felt like she was on the top of the world.

In time, having everything spoiled the princess and she became vain and superficial. Hope went so far into her vanity that instead of feeling grateful and happy, she took everything for granted and abused her blessings. She hurt many people with her selfish ways. She even hurt the prince she was meant to marry.

One day she offended a fairy who was visiting the kingdom and she cursed Hope to be forgotten by everyone until she would learn the true value of her name. And so everyone forgot her, including her parents, her prince, her friends and all of her subjects. There was nothing else to do but leave and so she left.

She walked until the end of the kingdom and then she walked some more. Her sorrow was as long as the road ahead of her, her despair as deep as the deepest forest she had to cross. She cried a river and then she cried an ocean. There was nobody to turn to and so she turned to herself. There was nobody to talk to, so she started talking to the trees and to the sky. Someone had once told her that a princess should always hold her head up, or else her crown would fall. But Hope didn't have a crown anymore, her head was down and she herself was beginning to forget who she really was.

She passed through towns and villages but nobody wanted to offer her shelter. One day, she reached a small village. She saw some women at the river washing clothes and her attention was drawn to the coloured water around them. After talking to them, she found out that they were a village of carpet-weavers and they were washing some new carpets before selling them at the fair in the town nearby.

Hope begged them for shelter. One of the women said she and her husband needed help so they would take her in their house, in exchange for work. Hope gladly accepted and soon started her work as a weaver's apprentice.

As the days passed, Hope learned how to combine the colorful threads into patterns and make small carpets of her own. Her tormented mind found peace in the endless movement of the loom. Nobody ever asked her where she came from and she never told anyone anything about her past. They wouldn't have believed her anyway.

As time passed, she became a skilled weaver. While working, images from her previous life as a princess started to flash in front of her eyes, she began to remember all the beautiful things she had seen while travelling around her vast kingdom and she weaved them into her carpets. Soon enough, her carpets became more than just beautiful landscapes.

She remembered all the things she had learned about arts, science or governing the kingdom. She remembered all the stories her father used to tell her in his hope she would one day become a just and fair ruler. Her father had always tried to engrave in her heart and mind his ideals and values of an equal kingdom for all, but Hope had been too selfish to care. It became quite obvious to her after a while the reason why her parents had given her the name Hope. They had high hopes for her and she had disappointed them. But down in her small weaving room, alone with her threads, she was now starting to remember. She had nothing left to be vain about, so she found comfort in feeling humble. And she started to weave all her father's stories into the carpets. Stories of people living together in peace and harmony, stories of people being generous and kind to each other, stories of people being united as one. She didn't have much to give, but she could give hope to those looking at her carpets.

Hope's carpets had slowly become famous in the neighborhood town. There were common and noble men alike from all across the county who came to see and buy the carpets. Hope's master weaver had expanded his trade and had become quite prosperous. The whole village had benefitted from Hope's fame, as there were more and more buyers coming every day. People often asked her about the stories she was weaving into her carpets and she was always glad to share them, as they reminded her of her father. People from all walks of life were sitting together and listening to her stories. Noble or common, they were all in the same village, listening to the same stories, under the same sky.

One day, the Queen of the small kingdom where Hope was living sent a servant to buy a carpet for her. Hope recommended a carpet telling the story of a kingdom placed on the branches of the tree of life, where all people were connected to the flow of energy coming from the earth into each living being. The Queen felt inspired by her vision and invited her to the palace. She could see right away from Hope's manners she was no ordinary weaver, but she didn't inquire about her past. Instead, she introduced Hope to her own daughter, hoping the young princess would learn something from her. And in fact, the two girls became friends, and even though the young princess was a little vain, as Hope used to be, she felt very touched by her stories.

Hope saw a bit of herself in the young princess

and decided she would do anything she could to help her avoid all the mistakes she had made. The queen granted her the favour to live in the premises of the palace and offered her a small cottage. It may have looked like a cottage from outside, but inside, with Hope's carpets, it looked like a tiny palace.

One day, a letter came from the kingdom where Hope used to live that the King, her father, was organizing a big fair and was inviting craftsmen from everywhere to present their work. The queen insisted that Hope would go to showcase her carpets and that the young princess would go with her. Reluctantly, Hope accepted to go, her only comfort being that nobody in fact would recognize her. So she chose some of her best carpets and left for the fair, in a carriage.

She was feeling a bit overwhelmed at the thought of being close again to the people who once knew and loved her, to see her beautiful kingdom and all the landscapes that enchanted her as a child. She was feeling shy, a feeling Hope would never thought she would feel. She was also feeling scared at the thought that someone might actually recognize her.

She wasn't wearing diamonds and pearls and her clothes were quite simple, but as a skilled weaver, she had learned to weave her own clothes and simple as they were, they were unique, colorful and they always caught the eye. Besides, Hope thought to herself, she was accompanying a princess and she had been sent by the Queen. She had a sense of pride that she had gained the Queen's trust and respect through her own efforts and talent. She was quite famous by now and many master weavers had sent letters to the Queen saying they were looking forward to meeting Hope at the fair. Even if nobody else recognized her, she was still Hope, a master weaver.

The fair was grand and everyone loved and admired her carpets. Hope gained everyone's respect for her work. There were rumours that she would win the weavers' prize. The prizes were to be announced on the last day of the fair in a great ceremony.

When that day finally arrived, all the craftsmen were invited to the royal palace. By then, Hope was feeling at peace with herself, but still, the thought of seeing her parents and her friends was making her nervous. As she entered the palace with the young princess, she started to reminisce about all the happy times she had there, but also remembered the mistakes she had made. She was a different person now and even though it was still painful to remember her old self, she knew she had rebuilt herself.

Standing in the crowd with the other craftsmen, she was looking around at all the familiar faces of those she had once known. When her father entered the hall, her heart stopped for a second. He was now a King who had no children and his throne would go to his younger brother one day. Hope had to stop herself from running and throwing her arms around him. She also saw her mother standing by his side and Hope's heart melted in gratitude, remembering all the love they had given her through the years. Finally, the man who was supposed to announce the prizes was none other than the prince Hope was once supposed to marry. Her heart started beating really fast when she saw him, as she remembered the kindness and love he had showered upon her, while she was too selfish and proud to notice. They had all forgotten her and maybe she deserved it. Now she was back with her beautiful carpets, that some called magic carpets. "They would certainly take people on a journey," Hope thought to herself.

Many prizes were announced that night and towards the end the turn of the weavers' prize came. The prince said he had heard of a master weaver whose carpets were as magical as Aladdin's carpet, but that he had never seen them. He said he was looking forward to offer this prize and finally see if the rumors about those carpets were true. By then, everyone knew who the winner was. Hope's name was called and she had to go and receive her prize from the prince's hand. Her heart was pounding as she approached him. He smiled at her and gave her the prize, a generous sum of money, saying that he was ready to see the carpet.

When the carpet was rolled down from the ceiling, Hope could hear cries of admiration from the crowd. It was the same carpet that the queen had once bought from her, a kingdom placed on the branches of the tree of life, where all people were connected, living together in peace, harmony and equality. The same carpet, only much bigger. The colours were so vivid and the whole image so inspiring that the King himself stood up and came closer to look at it. The tree of life had always been a story close to his heart. The king could hardly believe that someone could bring this story to life in such a stunning way.

The prince was the only one who couldn't say a word. Hope immediately knew why. It was because on top of the carpet there were a few words weaved into it. It was something the prince had told her long ago, something nobody else knew. It said, "The world for lovers is no less than heaven." Words of love that Hope didn't really care for at the time they were spoken. She remembered them much later, while working on her loom, weaving the 'Tree of Life'. And somehow, those words became even more than words spoken by a man who loved a woman, they became words about lovers of truth, lovers of justice and lovers of peace. And Hope felt those words would describe her carpet the best, as the carpet was meant to picture an ideal kingdom, where love and unity among people would bring heaven on earth.

As all those around him looked mesmerized at the beauty of the carpet, the prince was trying to understand how a complete stranger would know words that were so close to his heart. Since he couldn't remember Hope, he had no memory of saying those words to anyone. His mother used to say them to him as a child and he had always thought that one day, when the right person came along, he would have had a chance to utter them. He had never been an easily impressionable person, and yet now he was dazed beyond reason.

Needless to say, the prince wanted to know Hope and soon enough he asked for her hand in marriage. The King, Hope's father, was so inspired by Hope's vision of the ideal kingdom that he asked her to be his personal counselor and in time he would often say she had become like a daughter to him. The prince's kingdom was an ally to Hope's, so it was only natural that the two kingdoms merged and created a new kingdom. Soon enough, Hope and her prince ruled over this greater kingdom and tried to recreate the vision she had depicted in the 'Tree of Life'.

Later, the kingdom where Hope had learned to be a master weaver joined theirs as well and their vision spread farther and wider.

A few years had passed and one day the same fairy that had cursed Hope long ago came to visit their kingdom again. Hope was weaving a new carpet in the palace's garden. The fairy came as a maid and brought her a tray with a glass of water. She commented on the beauty of the carpet and said how everyone who looked at Hope's carpets, noble and common alike, felt a sense of hope for a better future. Hope soon realized she was no ordinary maid and thanked her respectfully. The fairy smiled and taking her normal appearance told Hope she was pleased with the person she had become. She said the curse had been lifted because Hope was the one who added value to her own name, thus learning its true value. And thus Hope got everything she used to have, not by birth, but by merit. And after saying these words, the fairy disappeared into thin air.

Hope smiled to herself and realized that even though the curse had been lifted, nobody knew who she used to be and that was alright with her. She didn't feel like a princess, she would always be a master weaver. She had left her old vain self behind and she knew it was dust. It occurred to her that all those years since she had been back to her old kingdom, she didn't think about the curse at all. Her life was better than the life she used to have and it was what she weaved it to be.

HOME IS WHERE THE HEART IS

Inspired by true events

It was a sunny, autumn day in Los Angeles. Jane and her colleagues were just ending a conference on multiculturalism. As an anthropologist, Jane had always been fascinated by the Native American culture, by their myths and beliefs. She was leaving the conference with mixed feelings. The workshops she had attended had brought to the table the delicate issue of the Native Americans' extinction, always a sad subject. On the other hand, listening to amazing stories about a rich, deeply spiritual culture was very elevating. Jane had always been fascinated by the myth of the White Buffalo Calf Woman, a mysterious woman who had appeared to the Lakotas in ancient times and taught them about the deep secrets of life.

Bearing all these thoughts and feelings in mind, Jane and three of her colleagues went for a hike in the beautiful area of Lake Piru, a few hours drive from Los Angeles. It was a famous area among campers, close to the Santa Clara Valley. The four anthropologists had heard about a monument dedicated to the last Indian of the Piru tribe, who had died in 1921, and they were all excited to see it. They were supposed to follow a country road closed to cars, where wildlife roamed freely. They walked for hours and didn't see a single human soul, but there were many birds, wild goats and beautiful flowers everywhere. As they were going deeper into the Piru Canyon, they immersed themselves into nature. The sounds, the scents and the colours were very vivid and the whole area seemed completely unspoiled.

Jane and her colleagues were discussing the rich information they had received during the conference. There were some local legends saying that before the white people came, some Native American tribes had completely disappeared without a trace. Some people believed those tribes had used their connection to the other world to simply disappear from our realm of existence, so that they would be protected from the great danger brought by the white people. Those tribes supposedly had a deep connection to the

Great Mother, the creator of the whole world. They could see everything linked as one, in the great web of life. Jane could definitely resonate with those ideas. A New York resident for many years, she had grown up in the countryside and had always felt connected to the rhythms of nature. The thought of seeing the monument dedicated to the last Indian of that tribe was very touching to her, a reminder of a long gone culture, so close to her heart.

At one point during the walk, a colorful bush caught Jane's eye. It had small, red flowers and for some reason, Jane felt she should pick up some and later offer them at the monument site. The winding road was following a valley amidst high rocky hills and at one point, it opened up to a wide space that looked like a prairie, surrounded by high mountains. The monument was placed on slightly higher ground, facing the whole place. It was almost sunset and while the prairie was in the shadow, the rocky, majestic mountains were golden-red, under the last rays of sun. The whole area was breathtakingly beautiful and filled with an out-of-this-world silence.

The monument consisted of a massive round, white stone, that looked like a one-legged table. Next to it, there was a commemorative plaque dedicated to the last Piru Indian. The four colleagues sat in circle on the massive stone, absorbing the silence. Some of them felt like saying a few words and Jane felt like singing. It was more like a Native American chant, that she knew so well, due to her years of studying their culture. When Jane finished her chanting, she noticed that in the middle of the stone there were four small holes, placed in a square. She smiled to herself when she realised that she had picked exactly four small, red flowers from the bush, on their way to the monument. She placed a flower in each of the four holes and she smiled again at how perfect that moment was. Afterwords, she closed her eyes and allowed the silence to take over every corner of her being. Soon, she started feeling that the whole place was vibrating with life, that every little grain of sand, rock or leaf was pulsating with the same energy. And she felt like she was a part of it all. A sense of great peace and joy filled her entire being.

There she was, thousands of miles away from home, and yet she had never felt more at home than in that moment. She had never felt so free. The wind had started blowing very softly and she could feel it on her face. That sensation gave her a strong deja-vu. She could almost see herself running freely on that prairie. She kept seeing, with the eyes of her mind, the image of her riding a horse, the wind blowing her hair on her face, while she was smiling, in complete peace and harmony with herself. "If I am to believe in past lives, this is the moment to start," Jane thought to herself. It was just a quick flash, but it was as if it was recorded in a very deep part of her soul. And that flash had triggered so many wonderful emotions. It was like diving deep inside herself and finding a treasure she never knew she was looking for.

When she opened her eyes, she had the impression that the air was filled with honey. It wasn't just the smell, it was as if the air and the atmosphere were filled with love and that love was almost tangible and it felt like honey. It was love that was connecting all living beings and the natives knew that. They knew it from the Great Mother, because a mother's love is unconditional and sweet like honey.

Jane saw her colleagues taking pictures of the sunset and wondered if she should join them. She was amused at their potential reactions to what she had experienced. They would probably ask her if she had smoked an Indian pipe with the natives. But Jane wouldn't need any pipe, as she had always been naturally high, and for her that meant being intensely connected to the present moment and to herself.

On their way back to the car and civilisation, Jane and her colleagues were once again sharing stories about the natives, about the White Buffalo Calf Woman and her teachings. None of them had a flashlight and that meant they walked in darkness for hours. It was a warm darkness that felt safe, like a mother's womb. The sky above them was full of stars and the stars felt so close as if they could be touched by hand. One of Jane's colleagues remembered a story in a local newspaper from years ago, when a white buffalo calf was born in Wisconsin. A native prophecy had said that the mysterious White Buffalo Calf Woman would return one day and then there would be peace. The Wisconsin white calf was a sign to many that the prophecy wasn't just a myth. As a scientist, Jane had to be a bit skeptical, but she was now in a state of mind where she believed everything was possible.

She didn't know what the birth of the Wisconsin white calf meant, but she was feeling inspired to continue her work with even more passion, determination and love. Maybe the prophecy was true and it meant those times were truly special. Maybe there will be peace. But now Jane knew peace could only come from within. She knew that the feeling of being at home would always be with her, wherever she would go. And she wanted to help others find their own peace and their own home. Her experience had been mystical no doubt, but it was also deeply grounded in the sacredness of that land, a land that once belonged to the Piru tribe. Her tribe. Her home.